THE

GHOSTLY TALES

OF

THE
FINGER
LAKES

Published by Arcadia Children's Books
A Division of Arcadia Publishing
Charleston, SC
www.arcadiapublishing.com

Spooky America is a trademark of Arcadia Publishing, Inc.

First published 2021

Manufactured in the United States

ISBN 978-1-4671-9827-1

Library of Congress Control Number: 2021932536

Notice: The information in this book is true and complete to the best of our knowledge. It is offered without guarantee on the part of the author or Arcadia Publishing. The author and Arcadia Publishing disclaim all liability in connection with the use of this book.

Images used courtesy of Shutterstock.com; p.18 MCDesigns/Shutterstock.com; p. 42 Spiroview Inc/Shutterstock.com; p. 54 Jsbaileyut/https://upload.wikimedia.org/wikipedia/commons/2/25/07_28_09_093_edited-1.jpg/CC BY-SA 3.0/Wikimedia Commons; p. 64 PQK/Shutterstock.com.

Spooky America

THE GHOSTLY TALES OF THE FINGER LAKES

JULES HELLER

dapted from *Ghosts and Hauntings of the Finger Lakes* by Patti Unvericht

arcadia
CHILDREN'S BOOKS

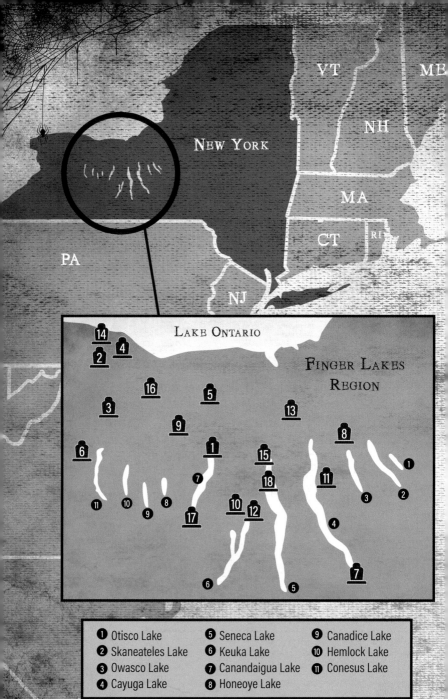

NEW YORK

VT

ME

NH

MA

CT

RI

PA

NJ

LAKE ONTARIO

FINGER LAKES
REGION

14
2
4
16
5
3
13
9
8
6
1
15
18
11
10
7
10
12
17
7
6
5

11
10
9
8
1
3
2
4
7

1 Otisco Lake	5 Seneca Lake	9 Canadice Lake
2 Skaneateles Lake	6 Keuka Lake	10 Hemlock Lake
3 Owasco Lake	7 Canandaigua Lake	11 Conesus Lake
4 Cayuga Lake	8 Honeoye Lake	

Table of Contents & Map Key

Skaneateles, New York

Introduction

Have you ever visited New York's Finger Lakes region, the area surrounding eleven long and thin lakes* that run side-by-side one another? Because you really should—they are truly a sight to see. Geologists use the term "finger lake" to describe narrow, extended, but still very deep lakes set within glacier valleys. In fact, the Cayuga and Seneca Lakes are two of the deepest lakes in the United States. The

---

* The eleven lakes, from east to west are: Otisco Lake, Skaneateles Lake, Owasco Lake, Cayuga Lake, Seneca Lake, Keuka Lake, Canandaigua Lake, Honeoye Lake, Canadice Lake, Hemlock Lake, Conesus Lake

Seneca is the deepest of the eleven Finger Lakes, measuring 618 feet deep—that's roughly seven times the size of a blue whale, the world's largest mammal!

Trust me when I tell you that room to move around is a good thing when it comes to lakes, especially if a sea serpent calls it his home, as one once did long ago in the deep darkness of Seneca Lake. *Or maybe not.* Perhaps the legend of the Sea Serpent of Seneca Lake is nothing but the seasick hallucinations of a handful of overworked sailors. One can never be too

sure of anything when it comes to the Finger Lakes, other than the beauty of their waters as they glitter and shine in the summer and the serenity of the snow as winter blankets the land.

Modern history of the Finger Lakes can be traced back to the early 18th century, when new American settlers came to the area originally settled by the Haudenosaunee Confederacy. Over hundreds of years, battles were fought, peace treaties were signed, and railroads and canals were constructed throughout the

Finger Lakes region, paving the way for the development of some of the biggest cities in Upstate New York. To the north, Syracuse and Rochester bookend the eleven lakes, with Otisco Lake to the east and Consensus Lake to the west. To the south, Ithaca and Watkins Glen sit at the base of Seneca and Cayuga Lakes, respectively.

Considering how vibrant the Finger Lakes region is, it's not a surprise that it has become a popular place for people to work, live, and vacation. The many wineries, breweries, and distilleries that are centered around Keuka, Seneca, and Cayuga Lakes are a major tourist destination, and the Geneva Music Festival hosts multiple concerts around the area every year. It would be fair to say that people lead very happy lives in the Finger Lakes. But sometimes, the legacies they leave behind take on a supernatural life of their own. There are dozens of opportunities within the Finger Lakes to see ghosts—for those who are brave enough to look. But you won't need to look hard. Certain places maintain a very ghostly energy, like static in the air just waiting to give you a shock! So dive into these pages as we take a journey through the Finger Lakes, stopping at all the most haunted places.

Secret Societies and Historic Treaties

The Ontario County Courthouse in Canandaigua, New York was originally built in 1794, and ever since then, it's been the home of legal debate for everything from parking tickets to murder trials. But perhaps the most interesting affair that occurred at the courthouse involved a local brewer and a secret society known as the Freemasons.

The Masons, as they are also called, have been around for hundreds of years. Originally, the Masons were formed by members who shared similar trades; then over time, "lodges," or local clubhouses, were built all over the world, and membership as a Freemason became a silent mark of status. In fact, some very famous people have been rumored to be Freemasons, such as George Washington and astronaut Buzz Aldrin. There are hundreds of conspiracy theories about the Freemasons, though it's important to note that many are unverified or lack evidence. But you don't need much verification from the residents to understand that in Ontario County, the Masons are most famous for what is known as the "Morgan Affair."

William Morgan was a local brewer during the 1820s.

He had been trying to join the Freemasons for years but kept being rejected. So, to get back at the Masons, he decided to write a book that would reveal all of their secrets. The Masons are famous for having secret passwords, handshakes, and other signals that are forbidden to anyone other than Freemasons, and Morgan's book threatened the very existence of the entire organization. But before it could be published, something happened to William Morgan that threatened *his* existence. First, he was arrested for theft. A friend paid the fine, and Morgan was released, but almost immediately, he was arrested again on a different charge. It was almost as though someone—or something—was trying to keep him confined.

After being arrested a second time, it seemed as though things couldn't get any worse for Morgan, but that they did. A stranger came to pay Morgan's debt, then had him released from the courthouse and escorted him to a mysterious carriage waiting outside. From that day forward, sightings of William Morgan were either scarce or unconfirmed, and he became the subject of many rumors. Many believe the Masons had Morgan arrested so they could keep his book from being published and then murdered him to protect the Freemasons' secrets. Others suggest the Masons finally let Morgan join their society on the condition that he leave his old life behind. One thing, though, is for certain: only William Morgan and the Freemasons know for sure what happened.

The courthouse was also the location of the signing of the Treaty of Canandaigua on November 11, 1794—an important event in early American history. This treaty was between the still relatively new United States and the Tribes of the Haudenosaunee

Confederacy, whose democratic government was inspirational to America's founding fathers. During the American Revolution, the Haudenosaunee Confederacy had allied with the British against the colonists, so this treaty meant a new era of peace between the nations. Naturally, the courthouse was the perfect place to make it official.

A memorial stone known as Treaty Rock sits in the courthouse square today and commemorates the event, but it is not the only remnant of that time. The ghost of Sagoyewatha, a skilled public speaker who represented the Haudenosaunee in treaty negotiations, is said to have been seen wandering around the building, muttering to himself. No one is really sure why, but perhaps he's practicing one of his speeches. If you see him, stop and have a listen. He probably would enjoy the audience!

2

Home Is Where the Haunt Is

What makes a building haunted? Need it be the setting of a particular person's last days, or can any old ghost or spirit just move on in? Does a ghost need a connection to a location, or can any wandering spirit decide to swing by for a haunting? This next story is about a house that's haunted by not one, but *two* former owners, and I wonder what brought them both back to stay. Maybe you can help me figure it out.

A man named Eastman Colby built a house in Ogden, New York, in 1811. He was one of the first homesteaders in the area, since this part of the state was still frontier territory. That meant he had to do a lot of hard, dangerous work by himself. One day, he was using an axe to clear a fallen tree from a road, when the axe bounced off the tree and hit him in the leg! Back then, such an injury could have meant the end for Colby. But Eastman Colby wasn't going to let a mere axe wound stop him from living his life. He recovered, finished building his house, and answered President Madison's call to fight the British in the War of 1812.

After the war, Colby sold his house to another veteran, Aaron Arnold. Arnold had deep ties to the Ogden community. He was deacon of a nearby church and supplied whiskey to local families from a liquor still he kept on the old Colby farm. Arnold may have had ties to other communities as well; it's rumored that there are old scrolls buried in the walls of the fruit cellar, holding private writings of the Freemasons—that's right, the same secret society from Chapter 1!

Arnold and Colby both died in 1859, but that doesn't mean you can't meet them today! The Ogden Historical Society has preserved their house just as it was, and that includes the two former owners' ghosts bustling around and making themselves known. If you visit, stay alert: you might hear footsteps behind you or feel like someone is breathing down the back of your neck. Don't fret, that's just Eastman Colby and Aaron Arnold welcoming you into the house where they've spent the last two hundred years!

Frontier survival, liquor distillation, and ghostly hauntings—there are strong spirits of all sorts at the old Colby house!

Genesee Country Village and Museum

CHAPTER 3

A Haunted Tour

This trio of tantalizing tales come from the Genesee Country Village and Museum, a living history museum with dozens of buildings that were moved together from locations across the state. The museum hosts classes and programs to teach people what life was like in New York State in the 1800s, with authentic artifacts and helpful historians ... but you want to hear about the ghosts, don't you? Well, let's take a walk around the village.

THE MURDER PLANT OF THE HOSMER INN

This peculiar story is from the nearby town of Caledonia. The Hosmer Inn was built more than 160 years before the village and museum were founded, and its spooky history is almost as old as the building itself. In 1814, a memorial rock was placed near the inn, over the grave of a soldier who had died there. If you visit the museum today, you can still see the rock, with this poem carved into it:

My brave lad he sleeps
In his faded coat of blue
In his lonely grave unknown
Lies the heart that beat so true.

It's a sad story, indeed, but it's not the only story the Hosmer Inn has to share. There is one far more mysterious. Right next to the memorial stone grew a strange flower that bloomed year after year, even though no other flowers like it could be found nearby! Think of it: one lonely flower next to a rock, blooming in bad weather and good, a strange bit of beauty in that solemn place. Locals called it "the murder plant" and left it right where it was, in case it was some kind of otherworldly phantom.

Almost seventy years later, the plant vanished, just as mysteriously as it had arrived. Could it have been the spirit of the unknown soldier, finding its way back into the world, fighting for life? Or was it simply a sturdy weed, flourishing for years as the soldier's body gave its nutrients back to the soil? I'm honestly not sure which explanation is less creepy!

Strange Sights and Smells at Hamilton House

The Hamilton House was a normal, unassuming home originally built in Campbell, in New York's Southern Tier region. When the house was moved to the Genesee Country Village and Museum, however, *nothing* seemed normal about the house at all!

Imagine walking through the slightly dusty rooms, freezing in place when you hear a rattling doorknob from just behind you. You turn but see nothing. Back in the hallway, you 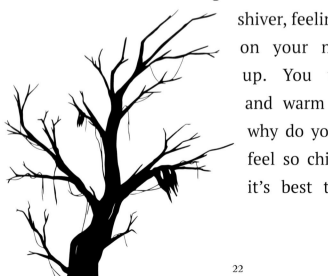 shiver, feeling the hairs on your neck stand up. You were nice and warm before, so why do you suddenly feel so chilly? Maybe it's best to go back outside and sit on the porch. You gaze out at the other buildings, thinking about which to check out next. Taking a deep breath of the warm summer air, your nose wrinkles. Is that . . . licorice? That's not something you expected to smell here.

But before you're tempted to investigate, you hear a sound from behind the front door. Someone is laughing in there. The laugh is high and unsteady, almost as though the sound is coming through a bad telephone connection. Except . . . you *know* you were the last one to leave the house. It was empty when you left. And nobody else has gone in since you came out to the porch. So . . . who's in there laughing? And where did the licorice smell come from?

Scents, sounds, and strange chills—they have a spook for every sense here at the Hamilton House!

SPIRITUAL VISITATIONS AT
THE OCTAGON HOUSE

The Octagon House is exactly what it sounds like. It's got eight sides, multiple levels, and lots of windows—a strange shape for a strange house. One hundred fifty years ago, it was the home of Erastus and Julia Hyde. Erastus had been a corporal in the American Civil War, but when he came home, he wanted to be a doctor. Julia was an ordained Methodist minister and a fine musician. But their shared passion wasn't for music or medicine. It was for spiritualism, the belief that the spirits of the dead can communicate with the living. Neighbors suspected the Hydes of holding séances in their oddly shaped house. (A séance is a party where the guests call dead spirits forth to communicate with the living.)

Whether Erastus and Julia Hyde conducted séances in the Octagon House is still anyone's guess, but there is no denying that the place definitely has a paranormal vibe. Visitors talk of doors that open and close by themselves and of footsteps that can be heard when nobody is around. And it's not just humans who find the place a little eerie: a stray dog was once seen wandering into the Octagon House, only to turn tail and run back out, whimpering. The dog stayed outside, barking, and refused to go back into the house.

What do you think it saw in there? Maybe it was the Hydes. Who can honestly say for sure? As we have just read, anything is possible at Genesee Country Village and Museum!

Erie Canal in the 1800s

Visions of a Victorian Past

Think about how people traveled in the 19th century. You might have a mental picture of horse-drawn carriages clattering over cobbled streets and dirt lanes, but did you know there used to be horse-drawn boats, too? It's true! When the Erie Canal opened in the early 1800s, draft animals like horses, mules, and oxen were the main power behind boats on the canal. The animals would walk down the "towpath" next to the canal, hauling barges and other boats behind them by long ropes.

Now, the Erie Canal is over 360 miles long, and animals need to rest just like humans. In 1825, a bright young man named Marcus Adams built a general store with a horse stable and tavern in the town of Adams Basin. Locals who lived along the canal and travelers alike could buy goods, rest, or eat there before continuing onward to their destinations.

Adams Basin was a busy and bustling area until the late 1800s. But by then, railroads had become so popular, people weren't using the canal to travel or ship goods, and Marcus Adams was forced to close his general store. It stood nearly empty for years but was restored in 1985 and became a popular destination. Why?

Because of the ghosts, of course! The place is full of them, and people love to try to catch a glimpse. Look to the windows of the upstairs rooms and keep watching. Sooner or later, a ghostly figure will come gliding past. On the main floor, be careful which rooms you enter; some visitors have lost their way in the halls and stumbled into a ghost party. Yes, you read that right—guests have found spirits enjoying an elegant Victorian evening party, complete with women in beautiful gowns and men wearing tailcoats which were a fashion staple in the 1800s! Who are these strange occupants? Could they be former travelers along the Erie Canal, resting ghost horses in the old stable, toasting each other with phantom glasses filled with paranormal whiskey? We may never know.

CHAPTER 5

Sybil, Guardian of the General Store

Think about the last museum you saw. Was it a new building? Brightly lit, with clean, white walls and floors and exhibits carefully displayed under sparkling glass cases? Well, the Historic Palmyra Museum in Palmyra, New York—which is about 15 miles south of Lake Ontario—is, shall we say ... *different*. For one thing, it's not just one building. There are five buildings within Historic Palmyra, but it's the

William Phelps General Store that is the one of most interest to the adventurous ghost seekers who come looking to catch a glimpse of its most famous apparition.

In the old general store, you can see the shelves where produce and dry goods were kept. Close your eyes, and you can imagine rows of glass jars, packed with everything from pickles to peppermints. Today, the shelves are empty, lit by one lonely lamp hanging from a chain. It swings gently, as if bumped by an invisible hand. If you visit, perhaps it's best not to linger long. But there's more to see in this building: boardinghouse rooms, a tavern, *and* a bakery!

Long ago, the William Phelps General Store was lively and bustling with customers and workers. Sibyl Phelps—the granddaughter of William Phelps, the original owner—lived above the store with her family. But unlike her family, Sibyl didn't really like going outside or seeing people, for that matter. She preferred to keep to herself and practice her piano. But Sibyl Phelps had one other hobby: communicating with ghosts! She was deeply

interested in spiritualism, just like the folks in the Octagon House. Maybe she preferred chatting up the dead instead of the living! So, it seems only natural that when she died, Sybil became a ghost herself. She lingers around the general store, and she doesn't seem to want to go outside any more now than when she was alive. She also still doesn't like being around people, either: her spirit has a habit of locking museum visitors in the downstairs bathroom!

You might see Sibyl walking through the kitchen upstairs as well or hear the ghostly sounds of her piano floating through the halls. The local spiritualist church still throws her a birthday party every year, and apparently she enjoys them. So if you ever attend one of Sybil's birthday parties, just remember: use the bathroom before you leave your house, just in case!

CHAPTER 6

An Unofficial Graveyard

About a hundred years before the Civil War, back in the late 1700s, western New York was considered part of the frontier—the border between the new American states and the wilderness. Settlers flocked to the area, buying up land for families, farms, and businesses. Unfortunately, many of them couldn't maintain the farms and fell into debt. The state government realized it had to do something for these people and, in 1827, established a "poorhouse," where folks who couldn't support themselves could live.

But this wasn't much of a relief for the people who lived there. Hundreds of people died at the Genesee County Poorhouse in the many years it was open. And what passed for "living" wasn't really much of a life at all. Instead of shelter and food, everyone at the poorhouse, including the children, had to work

the land. They chopped wood, farmed and even made coffins to earn extra money. The place was overcrowded, and when people got sick, it spread quickly.

That's pretty creepy, but wait, it gets better: they didn't keep very good records of where they buried all the bodies.

Sure, they know who died and what they died of, but there are rumors that bodies were buried wherever and however they fit. In the forest, in the basement of the main building—anywhere there was room, basically. Imagine that: anyone walking around the site today could be walking over dozens of graves without realizing it. No wonder people claim the place is haunted!

Some of the poorhouse ghosts aren't too friendly—a reminder of the harsh conditions people had to endure. One former nurse's ghost wanders the halls, pulling visitors' hair and sometimes even pushing them down the stairs. But other ghosts are kinder, as I'm sure many of the people who lived there were. If you visit, you might hear a strange, raspy voice floating through the walls. That's George, the ghost of a friendly old caretaker. He isn't angry; he just sounds like he's coughing up a hairball. People have heard him grumbling and growling at night. The old-timey music he liked to listen to in life still drifts through the halls. Considering all the people that lived and died here, it's no surprise that some souls still remain today.

Ithaca, NY

The Skeletons at State and Cayuga Streets

Now, I'm sure you know about haunted buildings because you're reading this book. But what about haunted wood—the very thing most structures are built from! If you're scratching your head right now, let me tell you about the State Theater in Ithaca, New York, and its grisly, gruesome history. It all started back in 1815, when a master carpenter built an inn on the corner of State and Cayuga Streets. The Columbia Inn was a popular place for people to gather and stay, as well as a popular place for violence—even murder.

Of course, murder is bad for business. So the inn's owner decided to tear it down and sell the lumber the inn had been made from. A lot of it was used to build Carson's Tavern across the street. Not even ten years later, guess where another murder took place? That's right, at Carson's Tavern, built from the wooden bones of the old Columbia Inn.

That's when folks started thinking there might be something supernatural going on.

The people of Ithaca decided there must be a curse on the lumber that once held up the old Columbia Inn. They began steering clear of Carson's Tavern, too; even going around the block to avoid walking past it. So when it caught fire and burned to the ground in 1845, most folks weren't that mad.

One would assume that a fire would be enough to break a curse, but that apparently was not the case. The same year as the fire, there was a murder trial in town. A man named Edward Rulloff admitted to a wide range of ghastly crimes—even claiming to have killed two members of his family. But a lack of any real evidence meant that Rulloff found his way back into the streets—and even more trouble! Thirty years later, Edward Rulloff was convicted of murder in Binghamton, New York, and reportedly had quite the chuckle as he was led to the gallows. That was 1875.

In 1928, the State Theater was built on the same corner: State and Cayuga.

Many years passed again. Imagine that you're a construction worker in 20th-century Ithaca. It's been years and years since any of these old tales happened, and your only thoughts are on the renovation job you've been hired to do. The State Theater, built back in 1928, needs some updates, and your team is the one digging up the old floors. It's sweaty work, and you're looking forward to a break and a cool drink.

Thunk. Your shovel hits something unexpected, something harder than dirt. Your friends crowd around you as you gently brush the dirt away, only to reveal . . . *a human skull.*

After the resulting shock and confusion, the authorities are called to investigate. You find out that *two* skulls, plus a full skeleton, were lying there under the old floors of the theater!

You remember the story of Edward Rulloff, right? Were these bones some of his victims? As you start thinking through all the spooky stories you'd heard about this part of town, you can hear the creaky old wood of the theater shift around you. Just like the Columbia Inn must have sounded, back in the day ... where was it originally built, again? The corner of State and Cayuga Streets? That's—that's where you are now! That's where the State Theater was built! Are these skeletons part of the old curse? Maybe it's best you don't stick around to find out.

Daggers in the Dark

William Henry Seward was a dedicated abolitionist who helped President Abraham Lincoln ban slavery in the United States. Seward was a man of influence and privilege, and he was able to help freedom seekers escape slavery while avoiding legal troubles for himself. He made his house in Auburn, New York, a stop on the Underground Railroad, and his family helped many people flee from their captors.

One person Seward helped was Harriet Tubman, who considered him a reliable friend in the fight for freedom. While Seward was governor of New York, slaveholders asked him to send freed people back to their former captors in the South. Seward refused again and again. Seward's actions and political views made him many enemies. He was even a target of the same assassination plot that claimed the life of President Lincoln!

It's a dramatic story: on the same night that John Wilkes Booth shot President Lincoln at the Ford Theater, another assassin, Lewis Powell, walked toward Seward's home in Washington, DC. Seward was a good friend of the president and a member of his government, and the conspirators wanted to strike down both of these powerful men at once. Powell knew he had a good chance to kill Seward, who was stuck in a sickbed recovering from a bad carriage accident. With a broken arm and jaw, it wasn't likely Seward would be able to defend himself.

To get into the house, Powell pretended to have medicine for Seward. His story worked, and he was able to get inside and up to the second floor. Then things started going wrong for him. First, his gun jammed, so he couldn't shoot anyone. Then there were more people in the house than he had planned for. Two of Seward's sons, an army nurse, and a

messenger all got in the assassin's way. Powell fought his way to Seward's sickbed with a knife, intending to complete his mission.

But luck was still not on his side. Remember how Seward was recovering from a broken jaw? His doctor had made a metal and leather brace for his chin to help him heal properly. When Powell tried to stab Seward, his knife couldn't get all the way past the brace. Powell's attack was ferocious but not fatal, and by this point, he had been slowed down enough that the police arrived to arrest him.

After the action was done, five men had injuries, including Seward himself, but the only death that night was President Lincoln at the Ford Theater. The murderous conspirators were tried and executed for their part in President Lincoln's assassination, but Seward healed from his wounds and continued his work in government.

The couch where Seward breathed his last breath is still here at the house in Auburn, as are many reminders of the incredible man . . . and of his friends, too. Many spirits have been seen in the house, but one stands out: the ghost of a black woman, leading another ghost toward the house until they both disappear from view. It's rumored to be the ghost of Harriet Tubman, helping other spirits to safety just as she did in her time on Earth, bringing them into her ally's house so they can finally find peace.

Valentown

Mysteries of the Old Mall

What comes to mind when you think of a shopping mall? Food courts, bright lights, and noisy crowds? Malls might seem like a modern thing, but there's one in Victor, New York, that has been around since 1879—and it's haunted. Valentown is a four-story building that used to house a busy shopping and community center, with lots of stores, a telegraph office, and even a grand ballroom for social events. Today, it's a historical museum and holds many memories—and ghosts—of the past.

If you visit Valentown, you might see and hear some odd things. Tools in the basement are said to move around without being touched. On the main floor, you can still smell freshly baked bread at the old bakery on the first floor, even though the ovens have been cold for more than a century. A magazine in a locked case upstairs has been seen to turn its pages with no help. And there's a piano and a Victrola—an old record player—that have been heard playing music without any helping hands. That is, without any helping *living* hands. Perhaps it's the work of a ghost the locals call Sarah.

They believe Sarah's spirit originates from sometime during the 1800s. She likes to watch visitors learn about the museum exhibits, and if there are young children in the group, sometimes Sarah will follow them, asking if they'll play with her. I bet she's *really* good at hide-and-seek! However, be sure to ask your tour guide to tell you about Valentown's most legendary tale: the murder in the grand ballroom.

Close your eyes, and you can envision the scene like you were there yourself. Around the year 1900, local dances were held at Valentown, and they were quite the attraction. Military bands were accompanied by a quadrille, which is like a square dance performed by four sets of partners. The women wore beautiful dresses, with loose sleeves, frilly petticoats, and corseted waists, while the men wore the

traditional tailcoats and trousers. As the story goes, a man arrived looking everywhere for his fiancée, only to find her dancing with another man. The jealous party crasher pulled out a revolver and shot his rival on the spot. That probably ruined the evening for everyone, don't you think?

Aside from a jealous assassin, the ghosts of Valentown really are quite friendly, but they're not always human, either. Valentown is also famous for a phantom cat who winds through visitors' feet. (And you thought all zombies were people, didn't you?)

CHAPTER 10

A Ghost Walks Into the Doctor's Office...

Stop me if you've heard this one before...

A patient walks into a doctor's office and says, "Doctor you have to help me! I feel like I'm invisible!"

The doctor replies, "What? Who said that?"

If you're groaning and rolling your eyes right now, perhaps consider taking pause for a moment. You'd be surprised at the number of people who have really seen or felt the presence of invisible people in the Oliver House Museum in Penn Yan, New York, which long ago used to be—you guessed it—a doctor's office!

The local medical practice was started by William Oliver, the son of one of the first doctors in Penn Yan. The village today is home to just over five thousand people and sits at the northernmost end of Keuka Lake, just west of Seneca Lake. William set up his house to have examination rooms where he could help his patients. Generations of doctors in the Oliver family practiced medicine from their home on Main Street.

Today, the place is a historical museum, but visitors hear and see evidence of bygone years all the time. Sometimes it's quiet whispers in the corners, but other times it's full-blown apparitions. Think about a visit to the doctor's office. Usually you sit in the waiting room until it's your turn, right? Imagine waiting in your chair, reading a magazine, only to look up and see a wavering figure appear out of thin air! What would you do? Would you try to ignore them? Talk about the weather? Read to them out of your magazine?

People think the ghosts are former patients of the doctors or possibly the Olivers themselves. Maybe they stuck around because it was a place they knew so well. Or maybe they wanted to keep helping others, as they had done in life.

By the way, here's another joke . . .

A skeleton walks into a doctor's office. The doctor looks up at the skeleton and says, "You're late."

Now *that one* was funny!

Wells College Admissions Building

CHAPTER 11

A Very Haunted Campus

Many colleges throughout the Finger Lakes region boast about their impressive programs, beautiful campuses, and long histories. But Wells College in Aurora, New York has a different claim to fame. It's quite possibly the most haunted college campus in the country.

In 1918, while America was in the midst of a deadly influenza pandemic, a few students died on the fourth floor of the main building at Wells College. There was nowhere to store their bodies, so the nurses picked a room and painted the door red. That's where they kept the bodies until their families could pick them

up and arrange for funerals. It was a good idea, as it allowed the dead rest in peace without disturbance. But not long after, the fourth floor was turned back into dorm rooms, and the lone red door was painted over. However, the red paint mysteriously showed through again and again, no matter how much they painted over it—almost like the door was bleeding. And to make matters worse, students who live on that same floor wake in the middle of the night to visions of a ghostly nurse with her hand stretched out to take their temperature!

As if that wasn't creepy enough, some years ago, two students—Ann and Mary—had returned from spring break and were settling back into their dorm. They heard a soft knock at the door and welcomed their friend Edith. Ann and Mary chatted about their vacations, but Edith seemed sad and quiet, not like herself at all. The others asked her what was wrong.

She said she was worried they would all drift apart after graduation. Ann and Mary hugged her and reassured her they would always be friends.

Edith left, saying she was going to visit their other friend Carol down the hall. But hours later, when she still hadn't returned, Ann and Mary went to Carol's room. Carol was just telling them that she hadn't seen Edith all evening when the three girls were summoned to the school office and given sad news: Edith had been killed in a car accident on her way back to the college from spring break. She

had never made it to the campus. So who—or what—did Ann and Mary see?

These are the stories that are passed down from student to student at Wells College, keeping the school "spirits" alive and well to this day.

A Ghost Is Born

It's quite true that the theater holds something for everyone. On the stage, you can see comedy and tragedy, life and death, sad songs and funny jokes alike. Don't believe me? Look no further than the Sampson Theatre in Penn Yan. Take a front-row seat to view the magic and mystery of the stage.

The theater was an impressive building back at the beginning of the 20th century.

It was built in 1910 and decorated inside and out. The main curtain on the stage even had a local piece of art on it: a hand-painted image of nearby Esperanza Mansion, a big plantation-style house with huge columns. Every day, rows and rows of seats were filled with audience members laughing and enjoying live stage productions, vaudeville acts, and silent movies.

For almost twenty years, the theater sold out show after show, until the growing popularity of a different kind of theater started to push them out of the limelight. Newly produced motion pictures were drawing huge crowds down the street at the Elm Theater, and the Sampson just couldn't compete with Hollywood. Soon, the curtains dropped for one last time, and the Sampson Theatre closed its doors.

In 2008, the Sampson was restored for historic preservation, and was listed in the National Register of Historic Places. Perhaps not surprisingly, some of the old cast and crew returned for a special encore—as ghosts! The most famous is the ghost of a Miss Eunice Frame, who was once a pianist at the Sampson. She loved music and theater, so it makes sense she'd come back, even though that took almost a century. But better late than never! If you visit, you might see her sitting near the stage or hear the sound of her piano echoing through the hall.

Actors oftentimes speak about "the spirit of the theater" to explain the magic and excitement of the stage. But if you visit that Sampson Theater and you're lucky, you'll experience the spirit of Miss Eunice, instead!

A Curse Upon
This House

What do you get when you add a headless corpse, a haunted mansion, and a possible serial killer? The strange and tragic history that exists within the halls of the Erie Mansion, that's what!

The Erie Mansion, which sits right along the Erie Canal in Clyde, New York, was owned by the Smith-Ely family. The Smiths were prominent doctors, and the Ely family owned one of the largest glass works in the world. But all the money and status in the world couldn't protect them from tragedy.

The Smith and Ely families traveled frequently between Clyde and New York City. After one trip, they came home to the mansion to discover a shocking sight: their cook, dead on the kitchen floor. Well, *most* of their cook. It's said that her head was never found!

From that point on, death just seemed to have its grip on the Smith-Ely family and the Erie Mansion. In time, six other family members died, under less gruesome circumstances than their poor cook, we're happy to say. But eventually, there was no one left in the Erie Mansion—no one but the ghosts, that is.

With no one left to speak for them—in *this* life, at least—stories began to circulate about the Smith-Ely family, particularly about Billy Ely, the mansion owners' son. Billy was said to be a bit too friendly with the young ladies in town and was known to drink too much. But a series of murders that occurred in both Clyde and New York City also led townspeople to talk about another possibility: Was Billy Ely a *serial killer*?

No evidence points to such a possibility, but that hasn't kept the locals from dubbing the Erie Mansion as "historically haunted." Among the many spirits people claim to have seen there, a woman in white is known to stand atop the grand staircase, while another woman dressed in black has been seen gliding through the walls.

Who are they? That remains a mystery— much like the legacy of the Smith-Ely family.

Voices From the Past

The Fowler Family Funeral Home of Brockport, New York, has been organizing funerals and memorials for generations, helping the living get through the difficult times and helping the dead find peace in the afterlife. As for said afterlife, the spirits that have passed through the doors of the Fowlers' business are somewhat mysterious in nature—even for ghosts. In truth, it's as though they didn't know they had died and are a bit confused of their whereabouts. Some even say you can hear the whispers of bewilderment coming from the dearly departed all throughout the funeral home.

"*Let me out!*" or "*Where am I?*" they're said to cry out. It's hard not to feel bad for them. After all, think about it: you would probably ask yourself the same thing if you woke up inside, let's say, a coffin, for example, wouldn't you?!

The funeral home also has an old doorway in the elevator shaft that is boarded up and

sealed off. But if you were to open that door, you'd see it's been boarded up on the other side! There's no actual way to get out of the elevator on that floor, and if you take the stairs up to the second story, there's no doorway at all—it's been sealed off for many years, as if to keep people out. Or maybe someone was trying to keep something else in?

Most people wouldn't think too hard about it and would say it's just old remodeling. But there are those who have heard voices coming from behind the puzzling, sealed entryway. Maybe it's just the wind coming through a hole somewhere in the roof. But given how many funerals have been held there over the years, would it really be a surprise if something more supernatural was at play?

You know, like a wily spirit determined to find a way out of the Fowler Family Funeral Home. Seems legit, right?

CHAPTER 15

An Unsettling Walk Through Town

There are buildings in Geneva, New York, that give off a strange feeling to the people passing by them.

Why?

Let's just say the locals have a hunch that an unknown force that attracts supernatural energy lingers throughout the town, invisible to the eye. Geneva is an old settlement town with a haunting record to match, make no mistake about it. Ghostly phenomena have been witnessed for centuries in Geneva, with the odd happenings usually blamed on the spirits of locals who died in the old buildings of years past. But sometimes there truly is no explanation at all for the things that happen around town.

For example, in 1796, construction began on a luxurious mansion with a beautiful view of Seneca Lake, but before it was finished, something went wrong. Nobody ever talked about why, but the people of Geneva did *not*

like that building. It made them uneasy to look at, and people whispered that it was haunted. Construction of the Seneca Lake mansion was never completed, and what was completed sat empty for thirty-some years, unfinished and unwanted. But eventually, the remaining structure was torn down, leaving only some tall trees in the yard and a beautiful view of the lake.

But not everything comes to such a serene conclusion, as was the strange case of the Dove Building.

Businesses in the Dove Building were successful for hundreds of years. It was the site of a popular tavern, some apartments, and even a fish merchant. But in 2004, the fancy restaurant there closed up very suddenly. So suddenly, in fact, that the owners left without their personal belongings! They just left everything right where it was, in the office, the kitchen, and the restaurant itself. Did something scare them off? What else could have made them get up and

leave without warning? Whatever the case, something is very much *not* right there!

Which brings us back to the town itself. Who knows? Maybe too many spirits have been disturbed as the town has grown and changed over the decades. Either way, if you ever feel the power of a supernatural presence, rest assured (or uneasy) that you're not imagining things.

CHAPTER 16

Keeping Ghostly Watch

If you drive through Rochester, it looks like a normal city. Buildings, trees, crosswalks, and ... a castle?!

Okay, not quite a castle, but the Main Street Armory looks a lot like one.

The armory has seen many different uses over the last century. Its indoor parade grounds have been used for every event from circuses to car shows and modified to act as both a professional sports arena and a temporary hospital. Mostly, though, the armory was a training facility for new recruits to the National Guard. Those castle-like walls saw hundreds of young faces go off to war, some of them never to return.

Other soldiers did return...but not in physical form. Ghostly gunshots sometimes echo through the dark, empty halls. Spectral "guests" have been seen shimmering in the corners of the old prison cells, guarded by ghostly sentries.

And then there's the coffin ceremonies. You see, when a soldier dies in a war, their unit will send their body home in a coffin, covered with an American flag. That way, their family can honor them with a funeral. It's traditional for the coffin to be sent to the local armory, where it stays under a twenty-four-hour vigil. That means another soldier, dressed in their best uniform, stands at attention next to the coffin for a full day, to keep harm from coming to the fallen. Have you ever tried to stand very still for a full day? It's really hard to do. Your muscles can get tired from standing still just like they do from moving around a lot.

But maybe it's different if you don't have a body to get tired. Because people have seen ghosts performing the coffin ceremony, too, out there on the parade grounds at night. Picture it: unearthly coffins draped in shimmering flags that seem almost made out of moonlight, with a ghostly soldier standing absolutely still nearby.

It seems the armory building has found a way to honor all of the soldiers who lived and trained there and bring peace to their memories.

CHAPTER 17

The Spookiest Bed and Breakfast

Would you spend the night at a haunted hotel? Visit the town of Naples, and you might not have a choice! The Naples Hotel isn't exactly what you'd call glamorous, but it has some very spooky stories to tell, if you're brave enough to listen. Naples is a very old town, established in 1789, and that's a lot of history to hold! Built in 1895, the hotel itself has seen over a hundred years of interesting people and events. Envision a building that's old enough to have seen big-wheel bicycles and horse-drawn carriages evolve into cars and trucks. Generations of visitors have passed through its doors, many unaware of what

waits for them on the other side. (No, not *that* other side!)

Some visitors of the hotel have seen apparitions. Others have smelled ghostly perfume from bygone times. One former owner was even driven out of the building, chased by unseen forces. And yet, people still rent rooms there! On purpose! Would you be so brave? Imagine calling the front desk for room service and having a ghostly attendant push his cart straight through the wall! Or having to wait for a strange mist to finish its journey past the ice machine before you can fill your bucket.

Through all this, every year, new visitors come to Naples, hoping to catch a glimpse of the past inside these old brick walls.

Seneca Lake

CHAPTER 18

The Sea Serpent of Seneca Lake

So far, you've read about secret societies, horrible murders, tragic tales, and ghosts. So it's only right that we end our journey through the Finger Lakes with a monster story for the ages—literally! You've made it this far, so we know you've got a brave heart and a strong stomach. But do you have what it takes to face down the Sea Serpent of Seneca Lake?

First, let's go back in time, *way back in time* . . . back to when gigantic glaciers from the last Ice Age carved the Finger Lakes into the land. There are eleven Finger Lakes, from tiny Canadice Lake all the way up to great Seneca Lake, which holds half of the water in *all* of the Finger Lakes combined. Now, Seneca Lake is deep—more than six hundred feet deep in some places—and when you have a lake that deep, you start wondering what it's hiding down there. (For example, Scotland's famous Loch Ness is just a wee bit deeper, at 745 feet deep. And we've all heard about the shy beastie that lives there!)

Close your eyes (if you dare), and you can see the sparkling waters of Seneca Lake shimmering in your mind. It's beautiful, giving off a stunning blue and silver radiance in the sunlight, with rolling green hills all around. But mystery lurks in the depths. The

Haudenosaunee Native Americans had legends about this lake. They said it was so deep, it had no bottom, and that a monster made its home in the dark depths. They treated the lake with great respect, but the white settlers didn't believe the legends. They should have listened.

For a time, all was peaceful on the lake. Many towns grew up around it, and it attracted lots of visitors, but nobody remembered the old legends. But on the July 14, 1899, all that changed. Are you still imagining the shining lake? Zoom your mind's eye in just a bit closer, until you can see the white shape of a paddle-wheel ship, steaming its stately way across the water. The ship is the *Otetiani*, and she carries passengers across the short northern end of the lake.

It's late in the day, but the sun is still up. Captain Herendeen is at his post, and it seems like a normal journey. But what's that over there? Look, a large shape in the water. The captain thinks it might be an overturned boat and decides to investigate, hoping to help any survivors he can find.

Except, it's not an overturned boat. Not at *all*. As the *Otetiani* paddles closer, the huge shape in the water starts to *move*. The people on the boat shout as they see a massive triangular head rise from the water at the end of a snakelike neck. The monster is roughly twenty-five feet long (still much smaller than the *Otetiani*), and after getting a good look at the ship and its passengers, it turns tail and begins to swim away.

"After it!" Captain Herendeen shouts, and the chase is on.

Why chase after this large and potentially dangerous animal? Well, Captain Herendeen knew how skeptical people would be when he told them the story, and if he could just find a way to bring the animal back to port in Geneva, people would believe him. The only way to do that would be to capture it, dead or alive. The *Otetiani* was just a small paddle-wheel ship, but Herendeen reasoned that if they could ram

the monster, they might be able to knock it out long enough to haul it to shore. So they chased after their prey.

Now, steamships aren't known for speed, but the *Otetiani* was the fastest of her kind. She was smaller than other steamers and had broken speed records for lake journeys, so her chances against the Lake Monster weren't bad!

Afterward, people gave different accounts of the chase, so I don't know how long it went on or how many times the ship tried to ram the Lake Monster. But eyewitnesses from the crew and passengers agree that they had crossed paths with the serpent at least once before it dived under the surface. Captain Herendeen thought the creature was gone forever. He turned the ship back toward shore, certain nobody would believe him.

But the *Otetiani* had done more damage than her captain thought, for passengers saw the body of the monster float up in the ship's wake. A large wound on its side showed them that they had indeed been successful in their hunt. The crew rowed their lifeboats over as quickly as they could and tried to get ropes around the body of the serpent, thinking they could tow it back to shore. But it was so heavy, the ropes could not hold it! The lifeless form of the Seneca Lake Monster slipped back under the surface one last time, drifting down into the depths, never to be seen again.

It's a wild story, almost unbelievable. Nobody since has found anything like the monster the *Otetiani* chased after. But think about how many witnesses were there that day. Besides the captain, pilot, and crew, there was a whole paddleboat full of people, including a local police commissioner, the president of the board of public works, a geology professor, and the manager of a phone company. How could these prominent people agree on such a bizarre story . . . unless it truly happened?

Occasional sightings of the Seneca Lake Monster have been reported since that July evening in 1899, but nothing up close, and nothing physical. Maybe the serpent was

the last of its kind, some kind of prehistoric holdout from just after the ancient glaciers carved the lake into the land. Maybe there are more monsters out there, hiding in the deepest parts of the lake. Maybe, just maybe, *you'll* be the one to find out for sure.

As we said from the beginning, people lead happy and vibrant lives in the Finger Lakes, and for the most part, so do the ghosts that also call this unique Upstate New York locale home. Maybe one day you will have a chance to visit and see one of the spirits for yourself. Rest assured, they will be waiting for you.

Jules Heller landed in New York State sometime in the last century and has been exploring the nooks and crannies of its landscapes—and legends—ever since. A graduate of Vermont College of Fine Arts, Jules has co-edited a collection of Halloween tales for young adults, and runs dozens of library programs for kids of all ages on every topic from mythology to memes. They have just moved into a hundred-year-old house in the greater Syracuse area, and are happily cohabitating with their new roommate, resident ghost Giuseppe.

Check out some of the other Spooky America titles available now!

Spooky America was adapted from the creeptastic Haunted America series, for adults. Haunted America explores historical haunts in cities and regions across America. Each book chronicles both the widely known and less-familiar history behind local ghosts and other unexplained mysteries. Here's more from the original *Ghosts and Hauntings of the Finger Lakes* author Patti Unvericht:

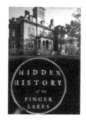